FLYING!

For Avery, my first little aviator.

May you soar with wings like eagles!

(Isaiah 40:31)

—*K. L.*

Published by
PEACHTREE PUBLISHERS
1700 Chattahoochee Avenue
Atlanta, Georgia 30318-2112
www.peachtree-online.com

Text and illustrations © 2009 by Kevin Luthardt

First trade paperback edition published in 2013

Book design by Kevin Luthardt
Cover design by Loraine M. Joyner
Composition by Melanie McMahon Ives

Illlustrations created in acrylic on Fabriano hot press watercolor paper; text typeset
in Baskerville Infant; title typeset in Microsoft's Georgia and enhanced in Strider's TypeStyler.

Printed and bound in November 2012 by Imago in Singapore

10 9 8 7 6 5 4 3 2 1 (hardcover)
10 9 8 7 6 5 4 3 2 1 (trade paperback)

Library of Congress Cataloging-in-Publication Data

Luthardt, Kevin.
  Flying / written and illustrated by Kevin Luthardt. — 1st ed.
     p. cm.
  Summary: A boy's simple questions about why he cannot fly lead to an imaginative
journey with his father.
  ISBN 978-1-56145-430-3 / 1-56145-430-3 (hardcover)
  ISBN 978-1-56145-724-3 / 1-56145-724-8 (trade paperback)
[1. Flight—Fiction. 2. Fathers and sons—Fiction.] I. Title.
PZ7.L9793Fly 2009
[E]—dc22   2008031116

FLYING!

Story and Pictures by
Kevin Luthardt

PEACHTREE
ATLANTA

Papa, why can't

Because, son,
you don't have
WINGS!

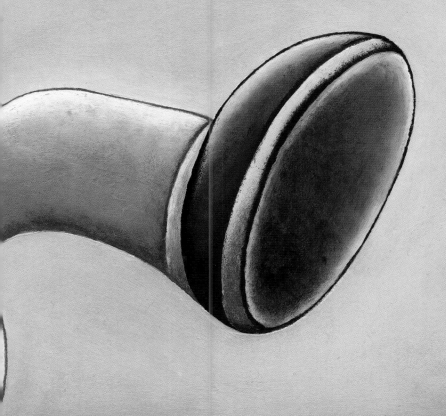

But…why don't I have wings?

Well, that's because
you have ARMS!

Well, why do I
have arms, Papa?

To hold up your HANDS, of course!

But why do I have hands?

Because, hands
are good for
GRABBING!

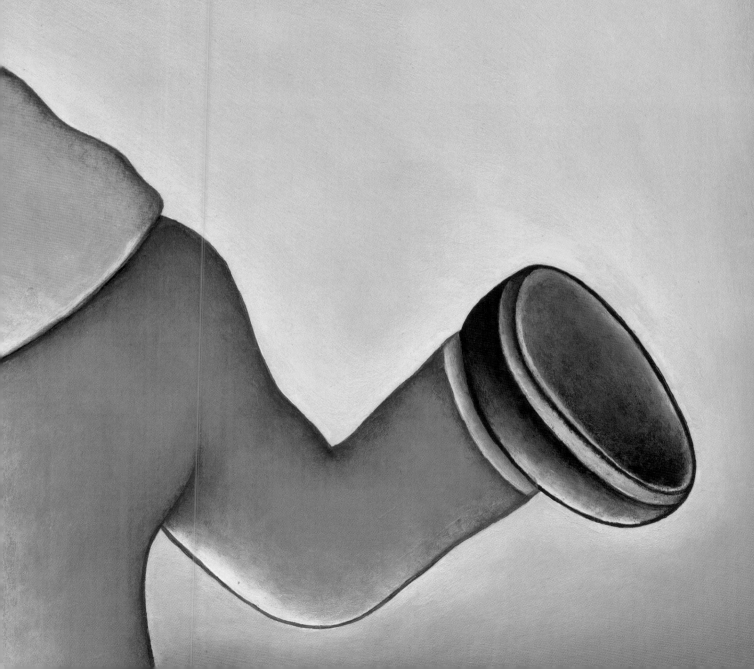

And SWINGING!

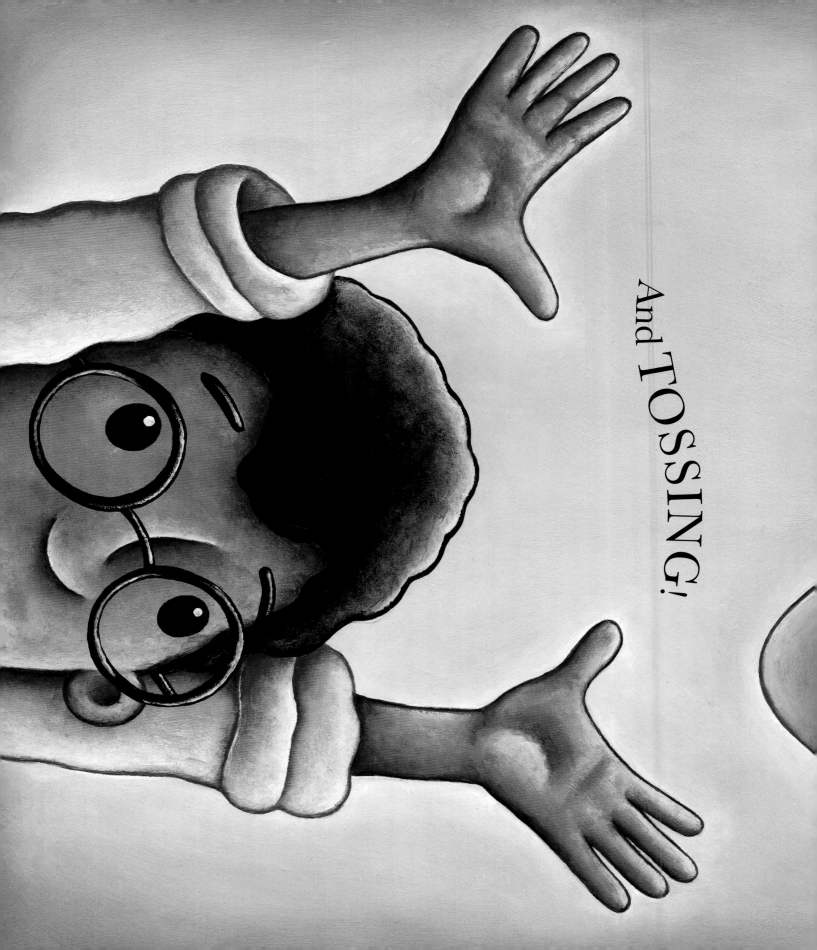

And TOSSING!

And…

I *can* fly, Papa!

Maybe I *do* have wings!

Maybe we *both* do!

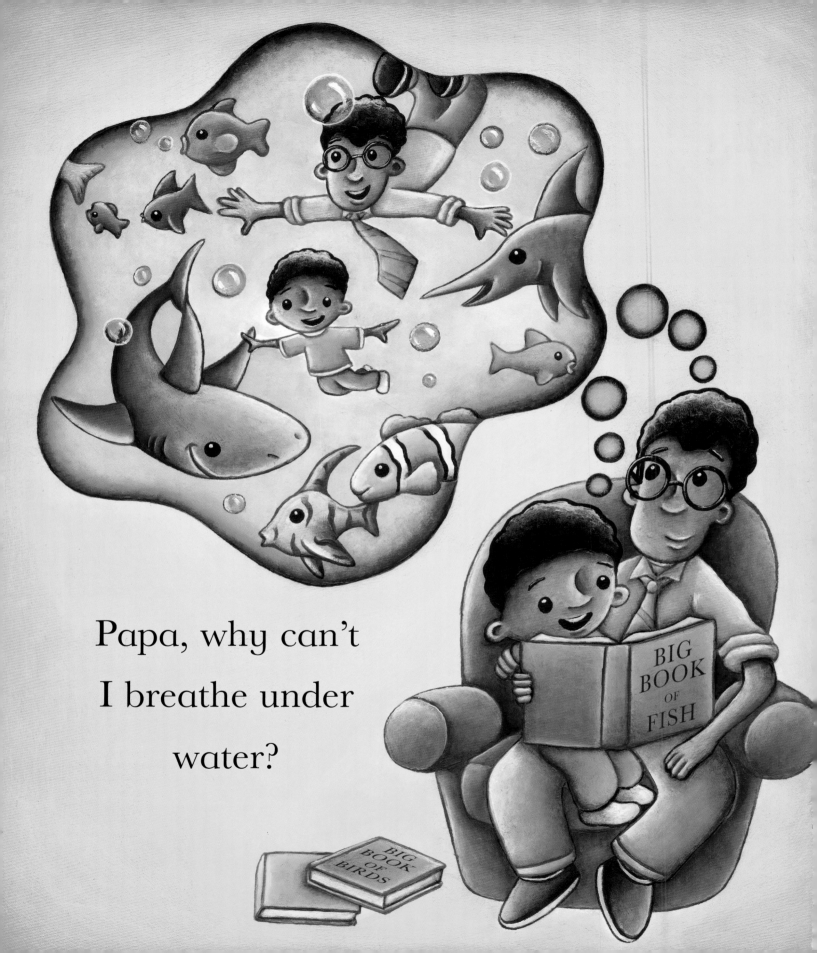

Papa, why can't I breathe under water?